KID KIBBLE

KID KIBBLE

Diana Hendry

illustrated by

Adriano Gon

CANDLEWICK PRESS
CAMBRIDGE, MASSACHUSETTS

For Toby and Baby Kibble

First U.S. edition 1994
First published in Great Britain in 1992 by Walker Books Ltd., London.

Library of Congress Cataloging-in-Publication Data

Hendry, Diana, 1941–
Kid Kibble / written by Diana Hendry ; illustrated by Adriano Gon.
—1st U.S. ed.
Summary: When Kid Kibble, the new seventh-grade biology
teacher, moves into their attic room with a skeleton and an
assortment of living things, Ned, his sister, and their mother
wonder if their bad luck with boarders is continuing.
ISBN 1-56402-413-X (reinforced trade ed.)
[1. Landlord and tenant—Fiction. 2. Teachers—Fiction.
3. Behavior—Fiction.] I. Gon, Adriano, ill. II. Title.
PZ7.H38586Ki   1994
[Fic]—dc20   93-47253

2 4 6 8 10 9 7 5 3 1

Printed in the United States

Candlewick Press
2067 Massachusetts Avenue
Cambridge, Massachusetts 02140

CONTENTS

Do You Like Fries?

Kid Kibble moved in to our house at the beginning of the spring term. Jess and I sat in the old hayloft and made a vow that he wouldn't stay. We raised our orange juice glasses in the air and clacked them together and Jess said, "Death to Kid Kibble!" And I said, "Slugs in his coffee!"

"I don't *really* want him dead," said Jess, lying back in the straw. "I just don't want him living *here*. He'll ruin my reputation."

I knew what she meant because Kid Kibble wasn't a kid at all, he was a teacher. Would you like to live with "Sir" in your home even if he did look like a big kid with a round face and round glasses and a grin like a jack-o'-lantern? And actually Kid Kibble didn't have another name anyway, so he had to stay with that one.

You see, he was the youngest of six Kibbles. There was Big Brother Tom and Big Sister Sue and Little Brother Ted and Little Sister Sal and Plus-one Harry and I guess by the time they got to Kid they just said, "Oh, here's another kid!" and left it at that. Kid he was and Kid he stayed. I don't suppose they ever thought of him becoming a teacher.

Kid Kibble was our eighth boarder. Every one of them had been a disaster but Kid looked like he was going to be the worst.

We started taking in boarders when Mom and Dad split. "It's that or sell the house, Ned," Mom told me. And we all knew the house was special. It was two hundred years old—old enough to have half a dozen ghosts, I'd guess, although we'd never seen one—and we didn't so much own it as it owned us. I think we were just the house's caretakers

until someone in the twenty-third century
came to claim it. It was a big house with old
stables outside and the hayloft above—our
hideout—and at the top of the house was a
nice empty attic. So we painted the attic room
white and moved in chairs and a bed and a
table and made it look cozy and then Mom
put a sign in the grocery store saying "ATTIC
TO RENT: APPLICANT TO SUIT OWNER."

The trouble was that Mom had no idea of how to choose anyone who would suit *us*. She would completely forget to ask important things like "Do you eat fries?" "Do you like dogs?" (we had three) "What time in the morning do you use the bathroom?"

"She had such pretty fair hair," Mom would say. "Such a nice little thing. I'm sure she'll be perfect for the attic." And the Nice-Little-Thing took three hours in the bathroom and had fifty boyfriends with loud and dirty feet who tramped up and down our stairs and had us all answering the telephone twenty-four hours a day.

After the Nice-Little-Thing we had Mr. Gooden. Mom took pity on Mr. Gooden. He knocked on our door and said he had nowhere to live. Mr. Gooden used to take his shoes off to walk upstairs.

"He looks as if he's apologizing to the stairs for treading on them," said Jess. And eventually Mom asked him if, as a big favor, he would keep his shoes *on*.

But the very worst thing about Mr. Gooden was that he loved machines. Any kind of machine—boilers, washing machines, clothes dryers, hair dryers, toasters. Mr. Gooden loved tinkering with them, taking them apart and putting them together again. Only he never put them together right. By the time Mr. Gooden left, we didn't have a machine that worked. No, there wasn't much that was good about Mr. Gooden.

And after him there was Scruffy Sue whose dirty dishes mounted to the beams of the attic, and Clean Kathleen who bathed six times a day and never said more than "hello" to us, and Bob, who *looked* like such a quiet young man but arrived with a set of drums that he practiced at midnight, and Nancy-the-Swindling-Swiper who stole our underpants off the clothesline and swore she hadn't, and Pure Patrick who was very worried about his health and kept telling us the preservatives in everything and the awful things french fries did to your brains. Mom felt sorry for Patrick because the cuffs of his pants were ragged. But we didn't. We thought a large plate of fries would do Patrick's brains a lot of good.

Anyway, you can imagine that when Mom said to us, very cheerily, over supper, "We're going to have a nice new boarder," both Jess and I groaned.

"What's the matter with him?" asked Jess at once.

"Nothing's the matter with him," said Mom. "He's a very nice young man. He's going to be a teacher at your school."

"A teacher!" Jess screeched. "How could you? I'll get teased all the time. I might as well *live* at school. He'll know when I haven't done my homework, and I'll never be able to swear again."

I let Jess do most of the talking in our house because when she's mad she talks fast and gets it all out at one time. When I'm mad I go into a kind of stutter. It happened now. "I'll n-n-n-n-never be able to ask a single fr-fr-fr-fr-fr- . . ."

"Friend home again." Jess finished for me.

"Ned! Jess! You're both being ridiculous," said Mom. "He's a very quiet and pleasant young man." (You could tell that she thought *all* teachers were quiet and pleasant and not Swindling-Swipers or Anti-Fries-Fanatics.) "This is his first job," Mom continued. "He's going to teach biology and he plays the trombone."

"Stinking snot-rags!" cried Jess. "Don't
you ever learn? Don't you remember Bob and
his drums?" Jess drummed on the table just
to remind Mom. Mom looked pained. "A
trombone," said Jess, as if Mom were about
five years old, "is just about the loudest
instrument there is! What else do you know
about him?"

There was a long silence in which it became clear that Mom didn't know anything about the new boarder except that he was a teacher, played the trombone, had nice little round gold glasses and his name was Kid Kibble. Shoes, glasses, a dimple, a name—there was never any logical reason why Mom thought a person was right for our attic.

"Kid Kibble!" said Jess desperately. "What kind of a name is that for a teacher?" So Mom told the story about Big Brother Tom and Big Sister Sue and Little Brother Ted and Little Sister Sal and Plus-one Harry and Kid. When she was done, Jess and I sighed. Mom was very good at learning useless information. She knew all about Mr. Gooden's terrible wife and where Scruffy Sue went on vacation and how much Bob paid for his drum kit, but about the things that make a person liveable with, she knew . . . NOTHING.

"Didn't you use the questionnaire?" asked Jess.

"How could I?" said Mom. "It's so rude."

Jess had made the questionnaire after Patrick. It went like this:

1. Do you like fries?
2. What time do you need the bathroom in the morning?
3. Do you take slow deep baths or shallow quick ones?
4. Are you in love? (In-love boarders were *the worst!*)
5. Do you like dogs? A lot? (This was because our three—Poops, Loopey, and Dash—liked everyone except the milkman. A great waggy, licky bunch.)
6. Do you have any strange habits?
7. Do you swipe underpants?

"It's not rude to want to know the facts," I said. I was very interested in facts at the time. I'd been given a book for Christmas called *Factfinder* and I'd started my own notebook for making lists of things.

Mom swept all the dishes into the sink in

an annoyed and clattery kind of way. It was
obvious we weren't going to get any more out
of her about Kid Kibble. (Unlike Jess, I sort
of liked the name. I thought it sounded like a
cowboy—Kid Kibble, Fastest Gun in the
West—and I added it to my list of names.)

Mom said Kid would arrive the next day, so
we spent the morning cleaning out the attic,
scraping Scruffy Sue's nail polish off the
carpet while Mom sighed over the marks on

the walls where posters—like boarders—had
come and gone. We all felt very cheerful when
we were finished, as though this nice sunny
attic would work like a magic spell to make a
nice sunny boarder.

None of us, not even Mom, were prepared for
the person who arrived the next morning. Even
Jess was speechless. We all stood in the hall and
Mom said, faintly, "This is Kid Kibble!"

The Worm Hunt

Kid Kibble had a skeleton hung over his left shoulder, three mouse cages slung around his waist, a trombone over his right shoulder, and a clutch of plastic bags in his one free hand.

"You don't mind Ernest, do you?" Kid Kibble asked, nodding at the skeleton. "He comes everywhere with me. I'd never have passed my exams without him."

"Well, no . . . ," said Mom whose life must be ruined by politeness. "I suppose he's been dead a long time?" (You could tell she was thinking that Ernest might clip-clop out of the attic one night on his bony feet.)

"Oh, at least two centuries!" laughed Kid Kibble, and he and Ernest rattled up to the attic. Rattled is the right word because besides the three cages, there seemed to be a lot of rattly objects in Kid Kibble's luggage. He paused at the top of the stairs. "Don't mind me," he called down. "It's just my big game traps."

Mom gave her small polite laugh as if she were used to having boarders who went big game hunting after school. We all went into the kitchen while Kid Kibble unpacked. Jess sat at the table and added another question to the questionnaire. It read, "Do you travel with a skeleton?"

"Biology equipment," said Mom, making herself a cup of tea. "That's what it is. Biology equipment for school. Things for teaching with."

At that moment there was a horrible wail from the attic as though someone had caught all his fingers in the door. We made for the stairs with Jess in the lead.

There, in the middle of the attic, stood Kid Kibble, trombone to his lips, blasting "Rhapsody in Blue" into Ernest's dumb skull.

"Just trying it out," said Kid Kibble giving us all his jack-o'-lantern grin and shaking trombone spit onto the carpet. "Does anyone else play? We could make a band."

"I play the violin," I said. "But I just started."

"Great!" said Kid Kibble. (I noticed he'd already knocked a nail into the beam and hung Ernest from it.) "We'll have a jam session."

"Don't get too friendly," Jess whispered as we went downstairs. "A teacher's a teacher, not a human being. You can smell them!"

"He wears jeans," I said. Jeans, in my opinion, are like french fries and dogs. A person who likes all three is likely to be very liveable with.

"That's just a disguise," said Jess darkly.

As it happened, it was rather difficult *not* to be friendly with Kid Kibble. After lunch he said, "Interested in some big game hunting?"

Now I don't think Poops, Loopey, and Dash have ever heard the words "big game hunting" in all their doggy lives, but they seemed to know it. They were there in a flash, Poops and Loopey sitting at his feet, thumping their tails and gazing up at him, while Dash ran around in excited circles.

"What are you going to hunt?" I asked. Kid Kibble was such an oddball that I half thought he might know of some ancient swamp where prehistoric monsters still lurked. Perhaps he was planning to bring the last dinosaur to a biology class. Jess gave me a don't-get-friendly kick under the table.

"Worms," said Kid Kibble, making them sound fierce as tigers. "I'm going on a worm hunt so I can dissect them with the seventh graders."

"I'm sorry," said Jess primly, "but we're both going out after lunch, aren't we, Ned?"

"What a pity," said Kid Kibble. "I wanted someone to pretend to be rain."

I couldn't stop myself asking what he wanted *that* for, even though Jess was making my ankles black and blue.

"Well, it's what birds do to get the worms out," said Kid Kibble. "They tap the ground with their feet imitating raindrops and the worms hear them and pop up."

I looked at Jess. I badly wanted to go worm

hunting. Calling worms up out of the ground reminded me of Indian snake charmers— maybe that's what they did on their drums, drummed large boomy raindrops. I thought Kid would know if I got the right moment to ask him. Jess shrugged as if to say, "do-what-you-like-but-I'll-get-you-later."

"Maybe I could come after all," I said, "and pretend to be rain."

"Let's see your fingers," said Kid. I spread them out on the table. "Oh yes," he said. "Very good for rain."

Jess snorted. "Oh, Sir!" she jeered, "you do have winning ways!"

"Jess!" said Mom. Kid said nothing. He went off to the attic to fetch jam jars for the worm hunt. (I think Kid told all his secret troubles to Ernest.)

We went down to the fields, taking Poops, Loopey, and Dash with us. Kid certainly liked dogs. I wondered if this might give him a good score in Jess's book. We squatted down in a shady corner on the edge of the field.

It was full of bluebells. And worms!

Kid marked out a square and I drummed
very lightly on the earth, pretending to be rain.
Those worms came up one after the other,
oozing up from their underworld, fat and thin
worms, straight and wiggly worms, all soft
and boneless and undressed looking, as if once
upon a time they might have had nice long
shells. Kid pulled them out of the soil and
dropped them into a jam jar.

It was like watching a conjuring trick.

"Why do they come out for rain?" I asked. "Do they want a drink?"

Kid laughed. "No, no," he said, "they think they're going to be flooded out down there."

Poops, Loopey, and Dash weren't at all interested in worm hunting. They ran around hunting strange smells that made all three of them quiver with excitement.

When we'd gotten several jam jars full of worms, we sat with our backs against a tree and Kid produced a candy bar from his knapsack. I knew he was worried about his first classes in the morning because every now and then he'd get out a book called *The Craft of the Classroom: A Survival Guide*. He'd look at a page and sigh and put it away again.

"The trouble is," said Kid, "that it's not so long since I was at school myself. I don't really look like a teacher, do I?"

"Well," I said, not wanting to discourage him, "if you wore a tie and flattened your hair down a little . . . " There was a shoot of hair just about dead center on Kid Kibble's head that seemed determined to stand up and wave to the world.

We finished the chocolate and walked home. Kid had packed lots of soil into the jars of worms and they'd wriggled down inside it.

Jess was really bad tempered when we got home. She was an expert at Black Looks.

When Jess gave you a Black Look you just withered into the earth like a worm going down. She was giving them all to Kid Kibble that day. And you could tell that although he was trying not to wither, he was feeling smaller and smaller by the minute. Jess kept calling him "Sir" in a nasty kind of way. "Have some bread and butter . . . *Sir?*" or "Sugar in your coffee . . . *Sir?*" It was the pause before the "sir" that did it, made it sound as if she was really saying, "Sugar in your coffee . . . *Slug?*"

"I think you can keep the 'sir' for school and call Kid 'Kid' at home," said Mom at last and at that Jess got up from the table and went out of the kitchen banging the door behind her.

I found her out in the yard, slumped in a deck chair with a hat over her eyes.

"He's not that bad," I said.

"He's awful!" said Jess from under the hat. "He's good and clean. I hate people like that."

"You like them b-b-b-bad and d-d-d-dirty,

I suppose?" I said. (The stutter came because I realized suddenly that I wanted Jess and Kid to like each other.)

"Yes, I do!" shouted Jess. "I do! I do! I do!" And she threw off the hat to give me a super Black Look. I shrugged and began to walk away. "And I'll get him too!" shouted Jess after me. "You just wait and see!"

I didn't have long to wait. About midnight there was a terrible scream from Mom. When I ran out of my bedroom I saw her standing at the top of the stairs clutching her nightgown. Her feet seemed glued to the carpet.

"Worms!" she said in a very small and shaky voice. "Worms everywhere!"

Well, that wasn't quite true. They weren't *everywhere*. But there did seem to be at least six, and the fattest six—unless they'd grown since Kid and I had collected them. They were wriggling around on the carpet as if wondering why it wasn't grass, and one of them seemed about to explore Mom's petrified toes.

I ran for a box and picked up the worms.

They were twitching in the light. Mom
unstuck her feet.

"Biology!" she said bitterly, and not for the
last time. "Why can't he teach geography or
history or something nice, like art?"

She put on her bathrobe then and we
marched up to Kid Kibble's attic, Mom
looking very haughty and annoyed, and me,
like a royal attendant, carrying the box of
worms.

Mom rattled the latch of Kid's door. I could tell from her face that on the way upstairs she'd prepared a long speech all about boarders not being allowed worms or girlfriends in their rooms after midnight, but it fell from her when we went in and saw Kid Kibble on his hands and knees under the bed, with a flashlight in one hand and a ruler in the other, searching for worms. The covers had been thrown back. The remains of the soil and one or two worms still wriggled on the bottom sheet. Kid came out, bottom first, a long worm held between finger and thumb.

Mom stepped back a pace. Ernest, in the draft from the open door, shook his bones like wind chimes.

"I really am very sorry," said Kid Kibble. "I don't know how these worms got out of the jars . . ."

But *we* knew, Mom and I.

"Jess!" said Mom. "And I'm the one to be sorry."

"A sort of practical joke, I suppose," said Kid

with a half-Halloween grin. "Not a snug-as-a-bug bed. A worm-squirming bed."

"Not a very funny joke," said Mom.

But I had the giggles by then and Kid caught them and eventually Mom stopped looking annoyed and began to giggle too.

"I'll go and get you a clean sheet," she said.

Kid and I crawled around the attic looking for worms and popping them back into the jars. Kid had to go out into the yard in his pajamas and get some more soil.

Just when we'd screwed the lids on the jars, I found one more worm about to wriggle into Kid's slipper and a big fat one curled up on *The Craft of the Classroom* that you couldn't see because the cover of the book was worm-color.

Then we made Kid's bed again and we all went to sleep, although it was about two weeks before anyone felt like walking around upstairs in bare feet.

And that was just the first thing that went wrong for Kid Kibble.

A Zoo
in the Attic

Things went wrong because Kid was trying too hard.

He was trying to be a good teacher. He was trying to be a good boarder. He was trying to be a good friend. And he couldn't get any of them right.

Jess didn't help of course. Jess put eggs in his boots and salt in his coffee and cotton balls in his trombone. Once, when Kid was out late, she dressed up Ernest in Kid's pajamas and put an old doll's bonnet on his head. Ernest looked odd enough to scare anyone. I wondered later if that's what set Ernest off, or if the house really did have ghosts and only Ernest could see them . . . but I'm jumping ahead of myself. Kid and Jess and the feud between them—that was the real problem then, not ghosts.

Kid never said a word about the salt and the eggs and the plugged-up trombone. Nor did Jess. They just didn't speak at all. They bowed to each other on the stairs or outside the bathroom door. One day, when it was pouring rain, Mom gave us all a ride to school and Jess was furious. As soon as we got there she leapt out of the car and ran up the walk. To be seen arriving at school with a teacher—well, you'd think that was Jess's reputation gone forever!

Even so, Jess got an A in biology that term, and she wasn't even in Kid's class. She was angry about that too. She said it was the most boring subject on earth, but I didn't believe her. I'd seen her reading Kid's animal and flower books and drawing pictures of the insides of elephants and the cells of a centipede.

And sometimes, when we were watching television, Jess would come up with some really odd question that had nothing at all to do with the film we were watching.

"Did you know that the worker bee has five eyes?" she asked me one night in the middle of a cartoon. "No, I didn't," I said. "Anyway, that's biology, *the* most boring subject!"

That shut her up all right. Actually I was a little fed up about Jess's A in biology. I'd only gotten a C.

"Don't worry about it," Mom said. "Jess has a scientific mind—you're more the arty type."

"Well, if Jess has a scientific mind, why does she hate Kid so much?" I asked.

Mom put on her dreadful I-am-an-understanding-person face. "Maybe they're too alike," she said.

Well, I didn't say anything to *that!* It made me think of Richard Dickinson at school and how everyone called him "arty" and how he didn't do anything but write awful poems that they always used in the school magazine when I was lucky to get half a paragraph in about some rotten school play. I hated Richard Dickinson.

The other thing that made me mad at Jess was the way she was always sneaking into Kid's room when he was out. Not that it was easy even getting into Kid's attic.

First of all there were the homework papers waiting to be corrected. They stood in little towers all over the floor so that Mom said the place looked like the remains of a Roman villa when just the bottoms of the pillars are left. Kid sat up late, night after night, grading papers and writing tomorrow's lessons, and Ernest dangled sadly to one side of him. Kid drank can after can of Coke and chewed tons of caramels as he graded papers, so there began to be a can mountain and a candy wrapper mountain. Mom didn't have the

heart to complain because Kid was working so hard. Sometimes she smuggled out a load of empty cans just so that Kid would have somewhere to put his feet.

Kid never threw anything away. He was a collector. And not just of cans and candy wrappers. Jess said, much later, that that should have been the first question on the questionnaire. "Do you collect things? Are these things alive?"

That's what I liked about visiting Kid in his attic—it was like going to a small zoo in your very own house.

"What are these things?" I asked when a small tank appeared in the attic. "These things that look like commas?"

"Can commas turn into frogs?" Kid asked. I liked the idea of this. A new kind of punctuation for English essays, frogs instead of commas, spiders instead of periods . . .

"I suppose you could draw frogs instead of commas," I began.

"Idiot!" said Kid. "These are tadpoles.

Their tails will disappear soon and they'll start getting legs."

Besides the tadpoles there were two white mice, a guinea pig, and a gerbil named Arthur (after our principal). There was also a goldfish bowl full of sticklebacks and a small army of wood lice that marched up and down inside a cardboard box and were fed on pencil shavings.

"What do you keep these for?" I asked Kid.

"They're a neglected species," said Kid. "No one seems to love them much."

An enormous spider had become a second boarder in the attic. He was cobwebbed in a corner just above Ernest's head. Kid had stuck a small sign beside the web that read "SPIDER AT WORK. DO NOT DISTURB." That was so Mom wouldn't dust him away.

Usually you could find Poops, Loopey, and Dash up in Kid's attic too. They'd be curled up on the bed since there wasn't space anywhere else. Kid often took them for a walk when he wanted to collect plants or more insects. They would lie on the bed looking as if they'd gone to sleep for a hundred years, but Kid only had to say "Worm Hunt!" and twelve furry legs scattered all the papers.

For a time, Kid had this gruesome experiment going on on the windowsill. He was feeding maggots on pieces of an old and moldy lamb chop.

"I want to test their response to light," said Kid and he showed me how to do it, putting

a single maggot on a blank sheet of paper, shining a light from one side and then tracing the maggot's route across the paper. "So you see I need to keep them fed," said Kid.

But Mom put her foot down. "Not in *this* attic!" she said.

Kid took to the backyard after that. He'd be out there trying to record the sound of crickets or growing tubs of dandelions for the school rabbit. Awful things began to appear in our fridge too. Bags of bulls' eyes from the butcher, the smelly heads of dogfish. Kid said you could learn a lot about the human brain from the brain of the fish because they were very alike.

"Biology!" said Mom when the bulls' eyes fell out at her feet while she was looking for a tub of margarine. "If only it were . . . "

"Geography, history, art," Jess and I chanted.

In fact Kid could probably have survived the classroom, Jess's withering Black Looks, and all the endless grading of papers. Where he really ran into trouble was when he finally met Mom's temper.

Mom has a temper something like a volcano. It whirls you up, flings you down, and goes off with a whoosh up into the sky. My theory is that it's being polite that gives Mom such a terrible temper. I mean being polite when she isn't *feeling* polite. Week after week goes by and there's Mom with her polite smile saying, "Oh yes, that's quite all right," or "Oh no, of course I don't mind!" when it *isn't* all right and she *does* mind. So all that temper works like a match on a slow fuse, or kerosene on a campfire and . . . BANG! WHAM!

The volcano blows!

I admit, Mom had good cause. You just don't expect a plague of locusts in your house and Kid had promised he would be very careful.

The locust experiment began when Kid saw our old sandpit in the backyard. Did anyone use it? he wanted to know. And when he found that no one did, he said it would be the perfect place for breeding locusts.

"They lay their eggs in a hole in the sand," he said.

"But in Africa," said Mom. "Not in the United States."

"It's a good spring," said Kid cheerfully. "They'll breed here just as well. When the young nymphs crawl out I'll take them to school and the children can watch them molting."

"Won't they fly all over the place?" asked Mom nervously.

"Oh no," said Kid confidently. "They can't fly. Not until they've molted five times. They don't have any wings until then."

So Kid got some locust eggs from the Insect House at the zoo and dug lots of holes in the sandpit and planted the eggs. For the first week we were all out there three times a day (Jess on the sly, of course) looking to see if the nymphs were crawling out. But in the second week, when the eggs should have been hatching, we forgot all about them.

And that was Ernest's fault.

Ernest
Takes Over

Something disturbed Ernest. Something disturbed him very badly.

We all had different ideas about what it was.

"I think Ernest may have lived here once upon a long time ago," said Mom, "and some memory of it has joggled his mind." (She didn't mention ghosts, but I knew she was thinking about them.)

"Joggled his mind and his bones," I said.

Jess said it was nothing as romantic and crazy as that. Had we noticed, she asked loftily, that Ernest had lost his little finger? All three phalanges of it.

"Phalanges?" queried Mom.

"The bones of his little finger," said Kid miserably.

"Well, obviously," continued Jess, "he wants it back."

I knew what Kid thought, because he'd asked me when we were alone.

"Do you think Jess . . . ?"

"Another one of her practical jokes?" I said.

"Well . . . I just wondered," said Kid.

I didn't tell anyone what I thought. I wasn't going to risk one of Jess's Black Looks. But I thought Ernest was allergic to unhappiness. I'm allergic to lots of things myself. Things like cheese and homework. And there was a lot of unhappiness around the house. Jess and Kid still not speaking. Mom trying not to mind about maggots and bulls' eyes and minding a lot. Kid worrying about Jess and his grading and Mom getting irritable with him.

Did I say something *disturbed* Ernest? I should have said something—or someone—*unhooked* him.

We got home one day and found him in the sitting room in front of the television.

No, it wasn't on, but all the same, it was
terribly spooky. Ernest's skeleton legs were
crossed and his head was tilted to one side as
if he were thinking very hard about something.

Mom turned the color of pastry and Kid
turned the color of beets because, after all,
Ernest was his responsibility.

"I'll take him upstairs at once!" said Kid.

"You do that," said Mom sitting down in a
hurry. "Ned, make me a cup of tea. And Jess,
if this is your idea . . ."

"I get the blame for everything in this
house!" screamed Jess, slamming out of the
room.

I half believed Jess was innocent because she did go to a lot of trouble whittling a piece of wood into a new little finger for Ernest. But it didn't work. Ernest was still very seriously disturbed.

Almost every day after that we found Ernest in a new place. Propped up on a stool in the kitchen, sitting at the dining room table, and once in the bathtub. I thought Mom was going to faint right away then, she gave such a scream.

I can tell you, we were all pretty disturbed too. I mean we'd gotten fond of Ernest, but Ernest-hanging-on-a-hook. Not wandering around the house. I don't think any of us slept well. We kept wondering if Ernest was going to walk in the night, and every little sound you heard made you think of bones rattling, skeleton jaws clacking.

Poops, Loopey, and Dash weren't just disturbed. They were scared out of their doggy wits. Whenever Ernest was off his hook all three of them hid under the kitchen table and shivered like it was the coldest December they'd ever known. And we didn't dare invite anyone over. I mean what would you say? "This is Ernest. He's just one of our boarders. We like strange boarders in our house." No. We just weren't up for it.

One morning Kid found Ernest sitting on the back of his bicycle as if he wanted to go to school with him. All Kid's usual cheeriness seemed drained out of him.

"No, Ernest," he said. "Back on your hook."

Mom said, "I think I'll have to ask Kid to leave. And Ernest."

"You can't do that," I said. "It's just not fair. It's not Kid's fault. He's really trying hard to be a good boarder."

"Well, he's not doing very well," said Mom.

"Give him another chance," I said. Suddenly the thought of our house without Kid in the attic made me feel very lonely. "Ernest may settle down again."

"I want him to settle *up!*" said Mom. "Up on his hook!" But she didn't do anything about telling Kid to go.

You can imagine that with all this going on we completely forgot about the locusts in the sandpit molting into nymphs. Once they molted, twice they molted, three times they molted, four . . . and the fifth time they got wings.

I suppose it's possible that the plague of locusts could have gone somewhere else. They could have swarmed off to the the town hall, or the police station, or the library, or the school. Back to Africa even. But they didn't. They swarmed into our house with their armored heads and googly eyes.

And that *was* Kid's fault. Because the locusts got their wings on the very night that Kid had set up The Great Insect Trap.

The Great
Insect Trap

The Great Insect Trap was very simple and horribly successful. It consisted of Kid creeping downstairs when everyone was asleep, opening the kitchen window, and leaving the light on. Kid had intended to get up while it was still dark, before anyone else was out of bed, and catch all the insects that had been drawn in by the electric light. Then he would take them to school. But all the homework he had to correct made him tired. He slept through his four A.M. alarm.

Mom was Kid's alarm that morning. She was woken at about five o'clock by Poops, Loopey, and Dash growling, whining, and squeaking. She knew it wasn't Ernest, she said, because Poops, Loopey, and Dash don't growl, whine, and squeak about Ernest. They just shiver. So Mom picked up my bat and crept downstairs, ready to clobber any burglars. She saw the kitchen light on and practiced a stroke or two with the bat. There were intruders in the kitchen all right. But they weren't the kind Mom expected.

There was a horde of them! A savage horde, Mom said later—although Kid said they were just practicing with their new wings. A whole foreign legion of them lined the shelves, their eyes swiveling around and around like the lights of patrol cars. From the shelves the locusts dive-bombed across the kitchen, making a noise like a thousand zippers zipping up and down.

And there weren't only locusts. Two bats
hung upside down from the ceiling. Fat flies
glinted blackly on the knobs of the stove.
Lesser flies made a buzzing net over the sugar
bowl. Daddy longlegs—looking as if they'd
discovered a party—hopped and danced
everywhere, and moths, stunned by the light
they couldn't resist, staggered and fluttered
and bumped around like drunken sailors. The
kitchen looked like the airport would if every
imaginable flying object—every biplane,
triplane, helicopter, jet, sputnik, spaceship,
and flying saucer—took off at once.

Mom shrieked, dropped the bat, and fled upstairs with Poops, Loopey, and Dash at her heels. (*They* certainly weren't going to be left in the kitchen with all those locusts and the evil-eyed bats.)

Kid must have heard the thundering of fourteen feet pounding up the stairs and maybe guessed what was coming because he wriggled deep down in the bed, and Mom had to haul him up by that tuft of hair in the middle of his head, which was sticking out as usual.

"Biology!" Mom shrieked.

"What about it?" Kid yelped because the top of his head hurt so much.

"It's everywhere!" cried Mom. "I've heard of hands-on learning, but this is ridiculous!"

By that time all the noise had woken me. I'd been down to the kitchen, gotten tangled up in highway lanes of locusts traveling from east to west of our kitchen, and had had a bat drop from the ceiling and brush the nape of my neck with its wings. I got out of there quickly and raced upstairs, but by the time I reached Mom and Kid I was in such a state that I got the stutters and all I could say was "B-b-b-b-bats!"

"I know she is!" shouted Kid, leaping around on his bed. "Totally and utterly bats! Do you always wake boarders up like this? I can understand why none of them stay!"

Mom began chasing Kid with *The Craft of the Classroom* then. She was still so mad that all she could say was "Biology!" And all I could say was "B-b-b-bats!" Ernest, I noticed, was off his hook and seemed to be hiding under the bed, because I could just see his hand—the one with the missing little finger—peeking out.

Eventually, when Mom had run out of steam, she stopped chasing Kid and sank into a chair. "Insects!" she said. "Locusts! A plague of locusts! Kid Kibble, I won't have such things in my house, biology teacher or no biology teacher. Skeletons, yes! Drums, yes! Trombones, yes! Guinea pigs, white mice, gerbils—ALL are welcome!" (I thought she was getting a little hysterical.) "But NOT locusts!"

"Or b-b-bats," I said, because a bat brushing the back of your neck is not a nice experience, believe you me.

Kid had sunk onto his bed with his face in his hands. "The fifth molting," he said, "and the insect trap! Oh, stinking snot-rags, I forgot all about the locusts!"

I could feel the volcano bubbling inside Mom again. It swelled her up so that she seemed to get fatter and fatter before the explosion. The next minute she was on her feet, had picked up the goldfish bowl of sticklebacks, and poured it all over Kid's head so that he stood there, even his tuft flattened, with sticklebacks sticking all over him.

I grabbed all the jars of water I could find—
due to Kid's collecting habits there were plenty
of them—and combed the sticklebacks off him
and into the jars, while Kid hopped from foot
to foot and dripped and shook with temper
and wet because, as we soon discovered, if
Mom had a volcanic temper, Kid's was a
hurricane!

"You don't care about science!" shouted
Kid, reaching at least gale force eight. "And
your fridge is too small and there isn't a single
comfortable chair to sit in because those dogs
take up the whole sofa!"

"I *do* care about science," Mom fired back.
"And my fridge is only too small for bulls'
eyes and dogfish heads. And *your* skeleton has
made us all nervous wrecks!" (I'd counted
fifty-six sticklebacks at this point.)

"You don't care about insects," bawled Kid,
hopping onto the other foot as a stickleback
wriggled up his pajama leg. "You don't love
the insect world, and your fries are awful.
Stunted, skinny, frizzled little things instead

of good, fat, healthy french fries!"

"Fifty-seven, fifty-eight, fifty-nine, sixty!"
I said.

"I don't care for insects *in my kitchen!*"
Mom yowled. "And I don't care for you in my
kitchen and no one's ever said a word against
my fries!"

"Well, they're very nasty fries," said Kid.
"Almost as nasty as Jess's Black Looks. And
see how you've upset Ernest!" Kid lifted the
edge of the blanket to reveal Ernest hiding
under the bed.

"*I've* upset Ernest!" cried Mom, lava boiling out of her. "Think how Ernest has upset *me!* Think of your worms and your wood lice and your horrid, horrid locusts."

The sticklebacks were all in the jars now and I could see Mom eyeing the tadpole tank. It was a little big, even for someone with a volcanic temper. She went for the empty

Coke cans instead. "All these cans!" she yelled,
throwing one at Kid's head. "Haven't you ever
heard of a wastebasket? Wastebaskets are a
biological necessity!"

Kid picked up an empty can then. Any
minute now, I thought, and we could be well
into the Battle of Coke Cans. But just as they
were both taking aim, Jess appeared.

"I shut the kitchen window," said Jess calmly, "but I really can't catch all those creatures myself." She looked at Mom, red-faced and angry, and then at Kid, red-faced and dripping wet.

"Mom, you shouldn't beat up boarders," said Jess. "Kid is only doing his job. It might be nicer for you if he were doing art, but biology is much more interesting."

"Well!" said Mom, and again, "Well!" The volcano sizzled out as if several tons of water had been poured over it and Mom went down in size like a popped balloon. Kid too stood there looking astonished. Jess was the last person he'd expected to come to his defense.

"Come on, Sir," said Jess (only this time the "sir" was a nice affectionate kind of "sir") "you'll need one of these," and she handed him a butterfly net.

It took us two hours to collect the army of locusts in butterfly nets and put them into cages out in the stables. When they were safe we opened wide the door and the windows and let everything else fly away.

The bats, like Cinderellas who have stayed too long at the ball, went off in a hurry to find some darkness. Mom wouldn't let us eat breakfast until every inch of the kitchen had been scrubbed and swept clean and that included taking the dogs' baskets outside and giving the blankets a good shake.

That was my job, and I did Loopey's basket first. She had three blankets and when I shook the first something hard fell out and clonked on the ground.

At first I thought it was an old bit of bone. Then I looked at it more carefully.

"Ernest's finger!" I shouted. "I found Ernest's finger!"

Gerbil, Sticklebacks & Co. Unlimited

It really was Ernest's finger. A little chewed around the phalange (as Jess might say), but still a little finger. Ernest's.

Loopey, who spends most of the day lying on whatever bed she can find that isn't occupied, must have caught it when it fell through Kid's floorboards onto the bed below. I bet she thought it was raining bones from heaven. She's loopy enough.

Anyway, I gave Jess an old violin string and she managed to sew Ernest's finger back on.

Jess, having taken charge, made us all breakfast. She telephoned the school, too, and said that owing to an unexpected biological phenomenon in the kitchen (honestly, she was beginning to *sound* like a biology text book), Sir would be late for school that morning. I could almost hear the school secretary gasping with surprise.

"Thank goodness for that," said Kid. "I'll only have to teach three classes today instead of four. I can miss that awful bunch in 3B. They couldn't care less about biology."

Jess passed him a large bowl of raisin bran. "Some people just don't appreciate the world of the wild—flowers, animals, insects, and things," she said, giving Mom a minor Black Look.

"Some people," said Mom, giving Jess a blacker look back, "might appreciate a cuff on the ear."

"Particularly teachers' pets," I said because really, Jess was a little much.

As for Kid Kibble, he began to laugh. "All those l-l-locusts," he spluttered, "and b-b-b-bats and m-m-moths!" Then he gobbled up his raisin bran and pedaled off to school with the tuft of hair on top of his head sticking up like the tip of a submarine showing above water. We were all thoughtful for the rest of the day. Ernest stayed hooked on his hook. Jess and I were afraid that after the morning's row, Mom would decide that Kid had to go. Or worse, Kid would tell us he was leaving. You had to admit, Mom had cause enough. The nice young teacher had turned out to be—well, a real pest. And Kid had cause enough too, with all of Jess's nasty tricks.

"What made you change your mind about Kid?" I asked Jess later that day when we were up in our hideout in the hayloft.

"I suppose he wasn't good and clean after all," she said. "Just messy and worried like the rest of us. Really very human."

"Even though he's a teacher?"

"Well," said Jess forgivingly, "he can't help what he does, can he? I mean the president can't help being the president. I bet one day Kid will go off on a big safari and then we'll see him on television talking about it."

"I suppose all this has nothing to do with your being good at biology," I said. (Jess's latest drawings were of tadpoles turning into frogs.) But Jess wouldn't answer that question. She just dug me in the ribs and said, "If you were a worm, Ned, I'd dissect you into a thousand pieces!" Then she slid down the ladder from the loft and vanished until suppertime.

Both Mom and Kid were very quiet at supper. Mom was all polite again and Kid looked like he does when every class has been a failure. Eventually he said, "Look, I've been given a corner of the laboratory at school and I could keep the gerbil there and the mice and the guinea pig—and—well, I could even keep Ernest there!"

But at that we all protested. Ernest and

Kid—well, you just couldn't have one without
the other. And the house wouldn't be the same
without the wind chime of Ernest's bones to
rattle us to bed. So, that's how things turned
out. Two boarders stayed, Kid and Ernest,
and the others—Gerbil, Sticklebacks & Co.
Unlimited—went.

There were a few other improvements, too.
Mom bought a second fridge. It was to be the
boarders' fridge, Mom said, and boarders
could keep anything they wanted in it. Dogfish
heads, bulls' eyes—even ordinary food. And
Kid made french fries. Big, long, fat fries that
you could take up in your fingers and dip in
ketchup without getting sticky.

So by Kid's second term at school we'd all settled down together. Jess and I, trying to be prepared for boarders of the future, rewrote the questionnaire. Now it read like this:

1) DO YOU COLLECT THINGS?
   ARE THESE THINGS ALIVE?

2) DO YOU LOVE FRIES? AND DOGS?

3) ARE YOU IN LOVE?

4) DO YOU TRAVEL WITH A SKELETON
   (BESIDES YOUR OWN)?

5) DO YOU PLAY A MUSICAL INSTRUMENT?
   IF SO, WHAT?

6) WOULD YOU DESCRIBE YOURSELF AS

   a) GOOD AND CLEAN
      OR
   b) MESSY AND WORRIED?

After supper, and after Kid told us about the laboratory, and Mom about planning to buy a second fridge, everything seemed suddenly peaceful. Mom nudged Poops, Loopey, and Dash off the sofa and we all sat down—in comfort for once—to watch television.

Kid, as usual, had gone up to the attic to grade papers. But he must have gotten fed up with it very quickly, for suddenly there was that now familiar wail—the fingers-squeezed-in-the-door wail that made all three dogs droop their ears.

It was Kid on the trombone again, playing "Rhapsody in Blue" to Ernest.

I bet you are wondering about Ernest.

Well, Ernest stayed on his hook and never wandered again. Maybe Jess was right when she said he just wanted his little finger back; or maybe she was never going to tell us that she'd been the one to unhook him; or maybe Mom was right when she said that Ernest had lived in this house two hundred years ago and some memory (or some ghost) had joggled first

Ernest's mind, and then Ernest, off his hook. Mom had another theory too. "That row Kid and I had," she said with a laugh in her eyes, "I think it might have frightened the life out of Ernest!"

Personally, I still like my own theory, that Ernest was allergic to unhappiness. This is a nice arty idea in my opinion and I am thinking of writing a poem about it. After all, biology can't have all the answers, can it?

SURPLUS